Schrödinger's Cat

By
Eileen Schuh

Wolfsinger Publications Security, Colorado

Dedicated to my family, friends, and fans. I'm very lucky that you're all in the same universe as I am. Thank you for your support.

CHAPTER 1

Chorie slipped on her rubber gloves, grabbed the toilet brush, and sighed. She'd read somewhere that despite today's technology, she did more chores than the privileged of the middle ages. In other words...

She opened the toilet seat, held her breath, and squirted the blue cleaner around the rim...queens and princesses in the ancient world didn't scrub their own chamber pots...or their own floors. Hell, they didn't even suckle their own babies; wet nurses did.

She turned her head and inhaled deeply before leaning over the bowl to scrub. She thought of cold, dark, stone castles lit only by candles, smelling of rancid smoke...and mould in damp corners...and unbathed bodies. She thought of beheadings and public hangings. Of witches and knights and dragons...of untreated infections...of mothers dying during childbirth....

Of children dying....

She flushed the toilet and watched the water swirl down the drain. There would still be a brown stain at the bottom once the blue left. Probably some streaks on the side. There always were. A taunt. Because in some lab somewhere, a man who'd never cleaned a toilet in his life, decided the cleaner should be a thick blue. So thick and blue those who did clean toilets, couldn't see where they needed to scrub. She caught the sound of a moan over the whir of the water and stepped to the open door to listen.

Children dying....

Another listless whimper wafted over the back of the sofa, a soft cry of pain rising from behind a veil of sleep.

She flipped the lid closed without checking for spots and ripped off her gloves. She hadn't planned for her life to turn out this way. She hadn't wanted children, but Gus had. So, she'd conceded—on the condition she wasn't going to be a stay-at-home mom. She'd keep her career. Hire a nanny. Maybe a housekeeper. That's what the deal had been.

She left the aseptic aromas and cool smooth lino of the bathroom and made her way to the great room. Her stocking feet whispered against the plush burgundy carpet. The fridge kicked in with a low hum. The neighbour's dog barked.

She peeped over the back of the black leather sofa and caught the strange metallic scent of approaching death. The fever spots reddening her daughter's cheeks looked artificial—as if someone had brushed dry tempura over a thin pale parchment.

Krystaline was too young to realize the injustice of her pain. However, she wasn't too young to see the worry etched on her mother's face and understand that somehow, she was its cause. Krystaline would never have cried out had she been awake. So many times Chorie had seen the guilt smouldering behind the glaze of pain in her daughter's green eyes. "Mommy," she'd smile wanly, "I feel much better today."

Children dying...

A wave of guilt brought bile to Chorie's tongue. Sweat beaded in her cleavage and trickled into her bra. She loved Krystaline more than anything in the world, and shouldn't have been thinking about not wanting children. Shouldn't have been complaining to herself about how her life turned out. Those were evil thoughts considering...

Perhaps, she comforted herself, as she'd been counselled to do, these thoughts were simply her way of coming to accept the inevitable, the unfathomable.

Like when an old pet starts shedding, making mistakes on the carpet, smelling bad—so that when, two months later, it sucks its last breath, relief takes the edge off its master's grief. Perhaps that's what it was.

Or, perhaps, she was just finally going crazy.

CHAPTER 2

Chorie looked up as Gus came in the door. She closed the slick cover of her magazine, pushed it to the centre of the kitchen table, and wondered what it was she'd been reading—something about a movie star being mad at Oprah.

Gus kicked off his shoes, squiggled out of his tie, and hung it on the oak newel post. He wandered toward her, his eyes staring past her, through her. His lips drawn into a tight straight line.

Their counsellor had advised them to be more tolerant toward each other, more accepting of the differing ways people handle heartache. Chorie surmised the counsellor had no children because sharing their grief as a couple, wasn't going to happen, just as Gus' second visit to the counsellor hadn't happened.

After the funeral, Chorie intended on going crazy. She'd build a comfortable inner world in which to live. Gus would look at her with accusing eyes, say not a word to her, and seek out some other woman's arms for comfort. Anyone with kids would know that's what was going to happen.

Gus threw a stack of papers onto the kitchen table, turned his back, and plugged in the kettle. Chorie tilted her head. His strong, square shoulders strained against his white dress shirt. Although he was almost 50 and beginning to grey, he still had the angled physique that first attracted her to him.

He clenched his fists and laid them on the counter, one on each side of the kettle. He had the personality to go with the body, commanding respect with his deep, quiet voice, his intensity, and self-confidence.

At least, he'd once had all that. Now it was just pretence. His daughter was dying and he was a broken man. There was nothing left of him. Nothing left for her.

The kettle began whistling. He unplugged it, reached in the cupboard for a cup, and opened the black and gold ceramic tea canister. He pulled out a bag, dropped it in the mug, and poured in the boiling water.

He raised the cup halfway to his lips. "I'm taking Krystaline to Seattle," he said. He took a sip and began turning towards her. Chorie held her breath. Was he actually going to look at her? Have a conversation with her?

He stopped turning, though, and gazed out the window at the bright Alberta summer sun. It was well past six pm, but it wouldn't be dark for hours. The summer solstice had just passed. The longest day. June 21, Krystaline's birthday. Last week she'd turned eight. She would never turn nine.

"Seattle?" Chorie asked.

"I did some research on the internet," he said, dropping his eyes as he turned toward her. He set his cup on the table and reached for his papers. "There's a clinic down there offering a new experimental treatment. I'm taking her."

"She's too sick to travel," Chorie protested.

Gus slid the papers toward her. "I'm taking her," he repeated. He picked up his cup and walked toward his office.

"Don't you think this is something we should discuss? That I should have some say?" Chorie called.

She watched his back until he disappeared down the hall. She heard the soft click of the latch on the double French doors. She imagined him flicking on his computer, reclining in his leather ergonomic office chair, closing his eyes.

She picked up the papers and scanned them as she walked down the hall. They were pages printed off the internet. A medical protocol, the top page said, for treatment of a last resort.

She wrapped her fingers around the cool brass knob. Through the obscure glass, she could see Gus' undulating silhouette. She quietly turned the knob and pushed open the door. It was as she'd imagined, him lounging in his chair, his eyes closed—unshed tears. *Windows* blinking on the monitor, patiently awaiting his password.

"Ninety-eight percent of the information on the *Web* is false," Chorie said loudly.

"This isn't false," he said, only his lips moving. "I've crossed referenced it. Phoned them. They've accepted her for an assessment."

"There are lots of scams. People looking to take monetary advantage of those who are desperate."

"It's not a scam."

"I'll read it," Chorie said. As she walked behind him to the lounger in the corner, he pulled his chair forward and began tapping at his keyboard.

Chorie kept glancing at his profile as she read. It was so unlike him to consider something like this. He was a kind and gentle man and this procedure was anything but. She shivered.

"Gus," she said quietly, laying the papers on the coffee table. "We can't do this to her. After all she's been through already…."

"She wouldn't have been through all that shit if the doctors here had a half a clue!" he shouted.

Chorie cringed. It had been months since he'd had passion of any kind in his voice. She looked down at the papers and splayed her fingers over the top page. Something under her palm had stirred him.

Gus shoved in his keyboard and cradled his chin in his hands. "Childhood leukemia is curable! If the medical system here wasn't so ass-backward, she'd have been well by now!"

"Have you read this?" Chorie ventured. "Do you understand what it means? Do you realize the agony this will put her through? The dangers…."

"I'm not going to stand idly by and let her die!"

"They're going to remove all her bone marrow, her white blood cells. She'll be defenceless against any kind of infection…"

"I'm taking her. It's decided. I've booked time off work."

"Gus, you're not! At least talk to Doctor Melynchuk first."

"You talk. I'm done talking. Done with fucking talking! It's time someone did something for her!"

"They won't let you cross the border with a child if you don't have the mother's permission."

Gus pulled out his keyboard and leaned into the monitor. Chorie sighed, put her feet on the coffee table, and closed her eyes. She got it; he had all his bases covered. If she let Krystaline go to Seattle, it would be the Canadian medical system's fault when she died. If she didn't let her go, he'd blame her for killing his child. There would be a reason for her death. It would somehow make sense to him. He'd have a target for his anger, justification for his betrayal. Men liked to have reasons.

CHAPTER 3

Chorie heard the back door open and glanced at the clock. It was quarter after noon. There had been a time when Gus always came home about now. He'd drive up a few minutes after Krystaline walked in from school and make lunch for her. Sometimes Chorie, too, would skip away from the office to join them. She loved watching how father and daughter's faces would light up the moment their striking green eyes met. They were so much alike, those two.

"Mommy, you're home!" Krystaline's voice rang out. Chorie turned quickly and stared at her daughter. Krystaline was waving a crayoned picture at her. Smiling.

The girl shrugged off her jacket and let it slide to the floor as she waltzed into the kitchen. "Look! Do you like it?" she asked, holding out her artwork for approval.

Chorie could not draw her eyes from her daughter's face. Her cheeks were filled out; a healthy glow brushed her cheeks. Her tawny hair curled over her shoulders, shimmering, smelling like *Johnson's Baby Shampoo*.

"Don't you like it?" Krystaline asked. "We were supposed to draw a picture of what we think we'll look like when we grow up. See? I'm in a suit and I've got a briefcase because I'm going to be an accountant like you...Mommy? Mom! I even drew boobs."

"Are you...feeling okay?" Chorie stuttered as she took the drawing.

"Sure. I'm hungry. Where's Daddy?"

Chorie watched Krystaline clamber up on the stool at the eating bar. "It's a nice picture...."

"The other kids laughed at the boobs," Krystaline pouted.

"They're nice boobs," Chorie answered, placing her palm over the fluttering low in her abdomen.

"How come you're home today, Mommy?"

Chorie glanced at her day timer open on the phone desk. Her briefcase that she hadn't seen for months was unzipped beside it. Her suit jacket hung on the banister. She stepped toward the desk and heard the click of her high heels on the tiles. A copper-dyed curl fell over her face and she caught the almost-forgotten scent of lavender body spray. "I don't know," she murmured glancing at her diary.

For over a year, she'd not worn heels, or makeup, or perfume, and had written nothing in her book but medical appointments for Krystaline. Yet, today the page was full. She looked at her afternoon. She had a gynaecological appointment penciled in for herself at 1:30. "I guess I have a doctor's appointment."

"Oh yeah," Krystaline said with a sigh. "You're going for an ultrasound, to find out for sure if you're pregnant."

"I am?" Chorie said, turning quickly to her daughter.

"I heard you tell Daddy. I want a baby brother."

"I'll see what I can do," Chorie said quietly. She walked over to Krystaline, lifted her from the stool, hugged her tight and kissed the top of her head.

Krystaline was warm with beautiful long hair. There was flesh on her bones. Krystaline wrapped her arms around her mother's neck and squeezed. This was the way her daughter ought to be, not a limp, hot, bald, featherweight who whimpered in her arms and bruised beneath the touch of her fingers.

She answered Krystaline's squeeze with one of her own. "Kryssie," she whispered. "I love you."

"Daddy's home!" Krystaline said, struggling from Chorie's arms. She dashed to the back entry.

"Hey, Sunshine!" Gus called, ruffling her hair. "What's for lunch?"

"French toast. Please?"

Gus chuckled. "French toast it is," he said, taking her hand and striding into the kitchen. He gave Chorie a peck on the cheek then hefted Krystaline onto a stool and opened the fridge.

"Hey, Chorie," he said. "Do you want to go to Seattle with me next week?"

"Seattle?" Chorie said weakly.

"The Association of Architects is having its annual meeting down there. Thought you might like to join me."

"What about Kryssie?"

"I'm sure your mom will look after her for a few days."

"Say yes, Mommy! Please? I love it when Grandma looks after me."

"Because she spoils you rotten!" Gus chuckled.

"Seattle?" Chorie repeated.

"There's only three days of school left," Krystaline prattled. "Grandma and I will have so much fun."

"I must be dreaming," Chorie said.

"I'm only taking you to Seattle, not Paris!" Gus said as he pulled out the frying pan and a mixing bowl.

"What about that project you're working on? The deadline you were afraid you wouldn't meet?" Chorie asked.

"Stephen's got it under control."

"Stephen?"

"The new guy we hired. He's a whiz."

"You hired him?"

"Yeah. I told you that."

"I thought you said he was a pompous ass," Chorie protested.

"I didn't say that! Besides, as brilliant as he is, he has a right to be pompous. I can see him buying into the partnership in a few years."

"Wow. I must be dreaming," Chorie said.

"Kryssie, your mother's gone crazy," Gus said, cracking the eggs into the bowl. He added some milk and seasoning and began whipping. He glanced up at Chorie. "You'll let me know as soon as you can what Doctor Koo says?"

"It better be a brother," Krystaline said.

Chorie covered her eyes with her hands. Nothing was making sense.

"What's the matter?" Gus asked.

Chorie dropped her hands to her sides and squeezed shut her eyes. "I don't remember wanting another child."

"What do you mean? It was your idea!"

"Remind me why," Chorie said climbing on the stool beside Krystaline. She set her elbows on the counter, cradled her chin in her hands, and stared at Gus.

"You said it's now or never," Gus replied. He dipped two slices of bread into the eggs and pushed them under the foam with the fork. "You're over forty. You didn't want Krystaline to be an only child."

"Oh," Chorie said.

"Work is getting too hectic; you're not into it anymore. You want to focus on motherhood for a few years."

"I do?"

Gus turned his back and slid the bread into the frying pan on the stove. It sizzled and steamed. "Are you having second thoughts?" he asked.

"No, I think they're first thoughts."

"What do you mean?" Gus asked over his shoulder.

"I suppose it makes sense. Because, God forbid, should anything ever happen to Kryssie, I'd still have a reason to go on with life."

"That's morbid thinking!" Gus scolded, flipping the toast. "You've got to seriously consider taking some time off, Chorie. You're half-insane, I swear. Come with me to Seattle. You need the break."

"That's what I always liked about you, Gus."

He took a plate from the cupboard, slid the toast onto it, and set it before Krystaline. "Eat," he ordered, passing her the margarine and jam. "What did you always like about me?" He dipped two more slices of bread into the mixture.

"That you're tuned to my feelings. That you care about them. I don't think many husbands would even notice their wives were stressed, let alone do something about it."

"I'm just returning the favour," he said. He stopped what he was doing and stared into her eyes. "Look, Chorie, if having another baby isn't what you really want…If you're just doing it to make me happy…."

"No!" Chorie said, straightening in her chair. She folded her hands on her lap. "No, it's not that. Not at all. You're right; I'm a bit touched. I just need a break."

She looked up at the ceiling. Heard the toast sizzle in the pan. "Dear God," she mouthed. "Please don't let me wake up."

CHAPTER 4

Chorie heard the back door open and glanced at the clock. It was quarter after noon. She looked down the hall expectantly, not daring to hope Krystaline would walk in, wave a drawing at her, say she was hungry.

"Mommy," a whimper rose from the couch.

"Are you home for lunch?" Chorie asked Gus as he walked in and brushed past her.

"No."

Chorie sank to the floor in front of her daughter. "What, dear?" she asked, laying a palm on Krystaline's fevered forehead. Her daughter's lips were cracked. Her scaly, pale tongue swelled out between them. She smelled like a tin cup might if tipped to the lips to drain the last drop of a strong tea.

"I want to sleep upstairs in my own bed," Krystaline croaked. "Please help me up."

Chorie quit breathing. Was this it? Was this the end? Like the old farm dog that wanders into the bush to die?

"No," Chorie said desperately. "You have to stay here where I can keep an eye on you, sweetie. Is there something I can do to make you more comfortable? Are you hungry?"

"I don't think so."

"I could get Daddy to make you some French toast?"

"Maybe a little piece."

"You need to drink," Chorie said rising. "Would you like some water? Some ginger ale?"

"Maybe an ice cube."

"Are you too hot? Too cold?"

"No."

"Do you want your teddy bear? Your Barbie doll?"

"I want to see the sun shining in my window. I want to look at the ballerina picture on my wall—the one Grandma made me…." Her eyes slid shut and her head sank into the pillow. "The peddypont."

"Petite point," Chorie corrected.

Krystaline's eyelids fluttered. "Petite point," she said dreamily. Her lashes stilled, her fists opened. Chorie bent and peered at her chest. It was rising and falling, slowly, rhythmically.

Chorie straightened. Who was she kidding? Krystaline had only agreed to eat to please her. Anything that slipped past her lips would be vomited right back out.

Gus had the cordless phone in his hand when she entered the kitchen. He was punching in a number.

"Are you sure you don't want some lunch?" she asked. He abruptly tossed the phone onto the desk. Chorie followed it with her eyes, wondering who he'd been calling. "I could make us some French toast. Krystaline said she'd try some."

Gus pulled out a barstool, sat, and stared out the window.

"Gus," Chorie said, pulling a stool around to face him. "I had this dream that…everything was okay. That Kryssie was home from school for lunch. You made us French toast. Asked me to go with you to the Architects Convention in Seattle…."

"Well, while you're busy dreaming," Gus interrupted, "I intend on doing something."

"Is the Architects Convention in Seattle next week?" Chorie asked.

"Damned if I know. I'm too busy to think of going to any convention."

"Isn't Stephen there to help you?"

"Not likely! I told you he's a pompous fool! All he wanted was a free ticket in on a partnership. All talk and no 'do' that man!"

"So how is it that you're able to find the time to take Krystaline to Seattle?"

"I'll be working eighteen-hour shifts from now until then, including this weekend."

"Ah, I see. Gus, could you just look at me? Please, just look at me!"

Gus turned his head toward her. She could swear he was looking at the bridge of her nose.

"Gus, have I ever talked to you about wanting another child?"

His eyes wandered down to her chin. "No, you've only ever talked to me about *not* wanting kids."

"Oh. In my dream, I was pregnant. I felt kind of good about that."

"What the hell does that have to do with anything?" Gus shouted. He spun his stool around, stood, and jammed his hands in his pockets. "Why are you thinking about having another kid, when the one you have is knocking at death's door? You think you can replace her? Is that it? Like a getting a new puppy when Fido bites the dust?"

"Gus," Chorie said quietly. "It was just a dream. And in the dream Kryssie was well."

Gus walked to the patio door.

"Gus, I didn't make her sick. Don't treat me as if I'm the one killing your daughter! Don't believe evil things about me. I want her well as much as you do."

"Then let me take her to Seattle."

"The homecare nurse is coming this afternoon. I'll talk with her about it."

"Sure. You do that." Gus grabbed his suit jacket, flung open the patio door, and walked out.

Chorie watched him stride past the peonies, and quack grass, and dandelions. At one time, his garden had been his pride and joy. And Kryssie had loved working alongside him, digging her hands into the dirt. Picking up the weeds for him and placing them in the wheelbarrow. She'd started helping him the summer she'd turned two. She'd toddled around the yard after him, gazing up at him. Listening to his every word.

Gus disappeared around the corner of the house just as the doorbell rang. Chorie glanced at the clock. One p.m., right on the dot. The homecare nurse was definitely punctual.

~ * ~

The nurse removed the stethoscope from her ears. "She's very dehydrated. Is she not keeping anything down?"

"She won't even try," Chorie said.

"I'll start another IV. You remember how to look after that?"

"Perhaps she should be admitted to the hospital."

"We could do that for you. I know there's a palliative care bed available."

"Mommy, I'll try," Krystaline said thickly. Dry pieces of her lips clung to her tongue as she ran it over them. "Promise."

The nurse motioned Chorie into the kitchen. "Is she becoming too much for you?" she whispered.

Chorie shook her head. "My daughter would never be too much for me. It's just that…Gus is insisting on taking her to Seattle for some experimental treatment. He won't listen to reason. If Krystaline's in the hospital, perhaps he wouldn't be able to…."

"I see," the nurse said.

"I don't know what else to do," Chorie said, blinking back the tears. "Kryssie doesn't want to be in the hospital and I don't want her to be…." Chorie began sobbing. She turned from the nurse, took at stool at the eating bar, and laid her head on her arms.

"Surely Gus realizes the child's too sick to travel," the nurse said, patting Chorie's shoulder.

"He won't listen," Chorie sobbed. "He won't accept…He blames me. He found this stupid clinic on the internet…I have to do something!"

"What kind of clinic?" the nurse asked.

"I don't know. Some research lab…."

"Usually reputable researchers only accept referrals from medical doctors. Has Gus gotten approval from Doctor Melynchuk?"

"No! He's gotten approval from no one! Can you do something?"

"Give me the information on this clinic and I'll see what I can do. Since it's an American outfit, we might have more clout than if it were in Mexico or something. Are you still going to counselling?"

"Yes, but Gus refuses. So it seems like it's all up to me to hold things together. I do what I can to understand him and he does nothing back!" Chorie straightened and wiped at her eyes. "I try. I try talking to him. He turns everything negative! I had this dream, this wonderful dream that Kryssie was well and I was pregnant. But when I tried to tell Gus, he berated me for thinking I could replace Kryssie with another baby! It was just a dream, a nice, pleasant dream, and I wanted to share it!"

"I'm sorry," the nurse said. "Do you want me to start the IV or should I call an ambulance to take her in?"

"Mommy!" Krystaline called from the other room. Chorie quickly wiped her tears and blew her nose.

"Yes, dear," she said, returning to the great room.

"I'm thirsty," Krystaline said. "Could I try some ginger ale?"

"She's saying that because she doesn't want to leave home," Chorie whispered to the nurse. "In fact, earlier she asked to go up to her own room. She doesn't want to leave us…before…it's time…."

"I'll start the IV," the nurse said, opening her medical kit. "Get me the papers on that clinic."

CHAPTER 5

"Gus, listen to me! I want her to die at home, not in some hotel room in Seattle," Chorie said.

"Want who to die at home?" Gus asked. He dropped his briefcase and gave her a peck on the cheek."

"Krys...," she started, staring at his back as he walked to the fridge. She ran her hand through her hair and sniffed at her palm. Lavender.

"Chris, who?"

"I'm sorry. It was just a bad dream, wasn't it? Krystaline's fine, right?"

"Yeah," Gus said, slowly. He popped the cap off a beer and turned to stare at her. "As far as I know...."

"Good," Chorie said. "I'm sorry. You're right. I need that break. I'm going crazy I swear."

"You dreamed Krystaline was dying?" Gus asked.

"Yeah, but she's not. The dream just got tangled in my mind."

"Okay," Gus said. "Do you want a beer?"

Tiny movements flickered across her belly. "I can't, Gus. Not when I'm pregnant. In my dream, you were threatening to take her to Seattle for some experimental treatment. But, hey, it's me you're taking to Seattle, right? For some shopping?"

"Yeah."

"Good," she said as the doorbell rang. "Are you expecting someone?"

"It's probably Grandma, coming to sit for us. Didn't she say she'd be here tonight so we can get an early start to the airport tomorrow morning?"

"Yes, right. My mother," Chorie said, rushing to the front door.

Chorie opened the door. Her chin dropped. She didn't know how to say it without being impolite, but she was expecting her own mom, not Gus', on her doorstep.

"Hello, dear," the woman said, barely concealing her distain. "How are you?"

"Fine," Chorie whispered. She inhaled. The lavender scent was gone, replaced with a cold metallic smell.

"Are you going to let me in?" the woman cackled, laugh lines chiselling their way across her face.

"I'm sorry, Lila," Chorie said, stepping aside. "I was expecting... someone else."

"Really? Do you have frequent visitors? Someone I don't know about?"

"My mother," Chorie said quickly. "She's over here often. Helping out."

"Well, this afternoon it's my turn." She took off her 1970's jacket, unwound a relic of a scarf from her neck, and held them out to Chorie.

Chorie glanced at her watch. It was 2:30 pm. She'd been so sure it was evening. That Gus was home from work. That there was a roast in the oven for supper.

"Be a doll, dear, and hang these for me," her mother-in-law said, waving her jacket and scarf in Chorie's face.

"What day is it?" Chorie asked, taking the coat.

"Monday, honey. You *are* stressed like Gus said! What a dear of him to arrange a visit to the spa for you. I raised him right, didn't I?"

"The spa?"

Lila stared at her and then snatched back her jacket. "Dear, I knew you were stressed, but I didn't realize how bad off you were. You must call on me more often to help. I don't mind; you know that." She slid open the front closet and hung her jacket. "I phoned you not an hour ago that I was coming to sit and you had a spa appointment, massage and all."

"I thought I was going with Gus to Seattle...."

"Really? That's not the story I got," she said, brushing past Chorie.

"I'm not going to a spa when my daughter's on the couch dying!" Chorie said, racing after her.

"Don't say things like that!" Lila scolded harshly. "She's going to get better. Negative energy around here is not what is needed."

"I want you to leave," Chorie said. "I'm not feeling well. I have to lie down."

"You need a break, dear. Krystaline will be fine with me."

"She's on an IV. I have to watch...."

"I was a nurse for thirty years. I think I know how to monitor a drip. Go; you're going to be late. There's a hefty fee for not showing." Lila peered over the back of the sofa, her feet a good six inches back from her nose, as if afraid she'd catch death if she went any closer to her granddaughter. "I swear she has better colour today and she seems to be breathing easier."

"What's it like to go crazy?" Chorie asked.

"Why would you ask *me* that?"

"Gus said you had a mental breakdown. What's it like?"

"I never had a mental breakdown! Nervous exhaustion, that's all it was. A few days rest and I was fine."

"What's nervous exhaustion like? Is it like you're in a dream and don't know what's real and what's not?"

"No! It's like you're tired to the bone and need to sleep or, perhaps, go to the spa. Go! Shoo!" Lila said, nudging Chorie toward the door.

~ * ~

Chorie sensed there was something wrong the moment she turned onto her street. She'd not enjoyed the spa at all. As stressful as it was to be at home with Krystaline, it was more stressful to be away from her. As she neared her house, she realized what had sparked her unease—the motor home was gone from the driveway.

She hit her remote and drummed her fingers on her steering wheel as the overhead garage door slowly slid up its rails. She turned off the car before it had stopped rolling and rushed into the house.

"Lila!" she called, not bothering to take off her shoes. "Kryssie!" She glanced at the empty couch, swung open the spare bedroom door, and raced upstairs. Krystaline's bed was empty; the bathroom was empty. There was no one in the den and the master suite was as she'd left it.

"Lila! Gus!" She raced down the stairs to the basement, flicking on lights as she went. No one was in the games room, or the half-bath, or the furnace room.

"Kryssie!" She ran upstairs, grabbed the phone, and dialled Gus' office. "Can I speak to Gus, please," she said panting. "It's his wife."

"I'm sorry. Gus is away from the office for a week. He'll be back next Tuesday. Is there a message for him?"

"Deanna. Is Deanna there? His secretary."

"I'm sorry, she's away, too. Can I help you?"

"Fuck!" Chorie slammed down the receiver, raced to the office, and rummaged through the filing cabinet. When she found the motor home registration with the licence plate number, she grabbed the phone and punched in 911.

"I need to report a kidnapping," she panted. "My husband has taken my daughter. I believe he intends on crossing over to Seattle. Please stop him! He doesn't have my permission to take her out of Canada!" She listened impatiently for a moment.

"No…No, there's no custody order. He just doesn't have my permission. Don't arrest him. Our daughter's dying. He's just stressed. He's not thinking properly. He thinks he's doing the right thing, but it's all wrong. Please! Stop him! Take the girl to the nearest hospital. She's on an IV. She's dying! She's so sick! Don't let her die! Don't let her die without me there!"

~ * ~

"Oh, it's you!" Chorie said, letting out a sigh of relief as she stared at her mother on her front step.

"You were expecting me, weren't you?" her mother chuckled. "I haven't got the wrong day or something?"

Chorie stepped forward, wrapped her arms around her mom, and laid her face on her shoulder. The comforting familiar scent of her mother's rose lotion mingled with her own lavender. "I don't know what to expect anymore," she whispered, fighting back tears. "Here, let me take your bag. Come in. I have a roast in the oven. Supper will be ready in about twenty minutes."

"Grandma!" Krystaline squealed, running down the hall and jumping into her grandmother's arms. "Did you bring that stuff?" she whispered.

"What stuff?" Chorie asked suspiciously

"Just 'stuff'," Kryssie answered evasively.

"It's just a wee something she asked for. A thing to pass the time while you're away."

"Would that be a *w-e-e* something or a *w-i-i* something, Mom?"

"Perhaps," her mother answered.

"Mom!" Chorie scolded. "You've been told not to spoil her! Aren't you afraid she's coming to like the things you bring more than she likes you?"

"The important thing to me," her mother said, taking Kryssie's hand and walking to the kitchen, "is that I like her."

Chorie sighed and wheeled her mother's luggage into the spare room.

She straightened the pillows, closed the blinds, and turned on the table lamp. She could hear Gus' low voice greet her mother and Kryssie's giggles and squeals. She heard the microwave timer go off.

"Emily," Gus was saying when she joined the family in the kitchen. "Have a chair. Thank you so much for agreeing to look after Krystaline for us. Chorie is in such a desperate need for a break. Has she told you the news?"

"News?" Emily asked.

"We're expecting again!"

"No! Really? When?"

"We just found out…"

"It's a stupid girl," Krystaline interjected. "I wanted a brother."

"A girl?" Emily confirmed, smiling at Chorie.

Chorie looked at Gus and nodded.

"Kryssie, girls are great!" Emily said. "You don't want a brother! Brothers are pests. You want a sister with whom you can share secrets, teach how to use makeup. Dress her up in pretty clothes."

Krystaline cocked her head and looked at her grandmother. "I do?" she asked thoughtfully.

"Sure!" Emily said, sliding into a chair beside her granddaughter. "Sisters are best!"

CHAPTER 6

"Where is she?" Chorie screamed, pouncing on Gus as he entered the motel room. She hammered her fists into his chest. "What did you do with her? Where is she?"

"Chorie, what's wrong?" Gus said, grabbing at her hands, his eyes wide. "Where's who?"

"Where's Kryssie? Where is she?"

"Is Kryssie missing?" Gus gasped, laying his hands on her shoulder. "Chorie, tell me!" he said, shaking her. "Is something wrong with Kryssie?"

"Don't pretend like you don't know!"

"But I don't know! Did your mother call? Is something wrong at home?"

"You're just trying to make me think I'm crazy, aren't you? So you can get custody! You're going to take her away from me! Is that your plan?"

"You're not making sense," Gus said, pushing past her. He grabbed the phone on the nightstand and began dialling. "What's wrong with Krystaline?"

"Don't do this to me!" Chorie screamed. She raced after him and pounded on his back. "How did you sneak her across the border? Where is she? The home nurse said the clinic wouldn't take her without a medical referral! You bring her all the way down here—for what? For what, Gus? I have the cops out looking for you! I'm turning you in! You'll face abduction charges if you don't tell me right now what you've done with her!"

"Emily, what's wrong with Krystaline? Is she missing?" Gus hollered into the receiver.

Chorie ripped the phone from Gus' hand and slammed it into the cradle. "Don't pretend with me, Gus! I know who you're calling! It was your own mother, wasn't it? Or Deanna? They're in with you on this! Trick me away from the house so you can take her!"

"Chorie, for Christ's sake!" Gus said, shoving her onto the bed and reaching for the phone. "I was calling your mom! She said there's nothing wrong with Krystaline. What the hell has got into you?"

Chorie looked wildly about the room. Her lavender perfume was on the nightstand. Her heels by the door. There was no sign of her daughter. Nothing. Her eyes came to rest on several shopping bags by the door, splashed with the logo of a Seattle shopping mall. She walked over to them and peered inside. There was the turquoise silk shirt she remembered buying. She pulled it out and beneath was the sexy red teddy she'd intended on wearing tonight. She'd been shopping all day—she remembered. She'd eaten pizza in the food court at lunch. She'd caught the wrong bus back and had been afraid she wouldn't be here when Gus returned from the conference.

She turned and stared at him. He was whispering into the receiver, his back to her. He gently hung up the phone and turned to her.

"Chorie," he said. "There's something wrong, here. I'm going to make an appointment for you to get in to see a doctor."

"A doctor?"

"You're…losing it, baby. Perhaps you can get a prescription to calm you down."

"I have a counsellor back home!" Chorie protested.

"You do?" Gus asked, screwing up his face.

"Yes, remember? When Krystaline was diagnosed…." Chorie trailed off, stumbled to the bed, and sat on the edge. She covered her face with her hands. "I'm sorry. I guess I don't have a counsellor. Yes, perhaps I should see someone."

CHAPTER 7

Chorie shifted uncomfortably in the chair and stared across the huge oak desk at the psychiatrist. He was ancient; Freudian, and so was his office—subdued lighting, thick, plush, royal-purple carpet.

She was surprised he hadn't offered her a black leather couch, although the dark recliner she was in came close.

He was pretending to read her file. She knew it was pretence because she hadn't said more than two words to him. A kindergarten kid could've read everything he knew about her three times over in under a minute.

She sighed and settled back in the chair. He wasn't going to offer her a cup of herbal tea like her Edmonton counsellor, or suggest she luxuriate in a bubble bath. He was likely to focus on ids, egos, and suppressed memories. Ambivalence, sexual frustration, penis envy.

He looked across at her with strange dark magnetic eyes. It was as though he could read her thoughts. "So what's happening with you?" he said in a deep preacher-like voice.

"I'm going crazy, perhaps am already there," Chorie said. His eyes were sucking at her innermost being. She was scared she'd lose her soul if she batted her lids.

"What makes you think you're crazy?" he asked, without shifting his eyes.

"It's like I'm living two lives," Chorie said. "Perhaps, I'm just having vivid dreams, but I don't know which life is the dream."

"Ah," he said, with a slow, knowing nod, as if she'd just revealed to him the secret of the universe. "Do you feel you're experiencing a multiple personality?"

"No, there's just one of me—two worlds."

"Ah," he said with another deep nod. He finally dropped his eyes, leaned back in his chair, and began chewing on the end of his pen. "Schrödinger's cat. Have you heard of it?"

"I don't know Schrödinger, let alone his cat," Chorie said.

"Schrödinger. Quantum physics."

"Oh, I thought you meant a cat-cat, a pussycat."

"I do."

"You do? Quantum physics has pussycats?"

He laughed loudly, like someone wanting to confirm they got a joke when they really hadn't. "Quantum physics has colours, flavours, and spins, too!"

"Right," Chorie said. She looked down at her hands, folded tensely in her lap, and wondered how she could leave without being rude.

"It has crazy people, too!" He again gave a belly laugh. Chorie kept her eyes on her lap and offered a small polite smile.

She heard his chair squeak and peeped across at him. His face was now deeply serious and he was leaning over his desk toward her, drilling into her soul with his dark eyes.

"Schrödinger's cat," he said. "A hypothetical animal that's caught between death and life by the mysterious nature of quanta. Quanta: subatomic particles that have two faces, neither of which they reveal until an observer checks in on them, and then they will reveal only one face at a time. Put a cat in a box that's rigged to kill the feline if face 'a' appears and not kill it if face 'b' appears. Drop in a quantum. What happens to the cat until the observer checks in on it?"

"Can the cat be the observer?" Chorie asked.

"No. It's a non-observant cat."

Chorie squirmed beneath his silent stare. She finally shook free of his eyes and looked at the ceiling. "What happens to the cat?" she whispered.

"Everett says it both dies and lives. Everett says anything that can possibly happen does happen."

His mesmerizing eyes and soothing voice had her feeling as if she was Alice, falling through the rabbit hole into Wonderland. Or perhaps more like the Wonderland caterpillar, sitting on a mushroom smoking his hookah. She'd never felt so unreal. She unclasped her hands, wiped a curl from her forehead, and closed her eyes. She'd read somewhere that if you wanted to wake up and couldn't, you should dream you were going to sleep.

She concentrated on her breathing and imagined a down pillow beneath her head, but nothing changed. The smooth leather of the chair still pressed against her back, the air conditioner still hummed. She opened her eyes. The doctor was scribbling rapidly in her file. She coughed and he kept writing.

"This Everett guy," she ventured loudly, "says it's possible to both die and live?"

"Don't sound so sceptical—so does the Catholic church."

"Oh....Everett thinks the kitty dies and goes to heaven to live?"

He threw down his pen as if disgusted with her question and leaned back in his chair. "Everett's *Many Worlds Theory*. How can the most important knowledge of the twenty-first century be so ignored by the world?"

"I don't know," Chorie muttered.

"It's this way. The observer looks in at the pussycat. At that moment, reality splits in two. The observer sees the cat is alive and life proceeds. Simultaneously, the observer sees the cat is dead and life proceeds—as least the observer's life does. It's generally believed there is little or no communication between these realities. There are, however, those who disagree. Perhaps these alternate realities are the source of inspiration, innovation. Dreams. UFO sightings. Ancient knowledge. Déjà vu. I believe you may be accessing two different realities."

"Oh."

"Here," he said, leaning forward and picking up his pen. "I'll give you a website address. There's some basic information on the theory and some recommended reading and links. Check it out."

Sensing she had a chance to politely escape his office, Chorie sprang to her feet and held out her hand.

"Sometimes if people can put a name to what's happening to them and realize they aren't alone with their experiences, it helps them adjust. They relax, relishing the fact that no matter what they decide, what experiences life throws at them, there exists another reality consisting of choices not made, roads not taken, and events not experienced."

"I see," Chorie said, as he slipped the paper into her outstretched hand.

He drilled his mystic eyes into hers. "Check it out," he whispered. "It's all pure science."

"What happens to those of us who can't relax into the experience?"

"If you find the situation unbearable, come back and see me. There are things I can do to help."

CHAPTER 8

"This last week's been tough on you, Chordelia," Adeline said as she dropped herbal tea bags into their mugs.

Chorie wiped a curl from her cheek. Her palm smelled of...zinc, perhaps. A harsh smell. Foreboding. "I had to give Social Services custody of Krystaline until the courts decide if Gus or I should have her," she offered. "I'm afraid the fact you're counselling me might not look good to the judge."

Adeline passed her a cup, took a sip from her own, and then nestled into the easy chair opposite Chorie. Although there was a small desk in the corner of the office, Chorie had yet to see Adeline behind it. Her counsellor didn't take notes, she voice-recorded. Her office was bright and airy. Her words, soft. Her eyes, pleasantly normal.

Adeline was the antithesis of the Seattle psychiatrist.

Chorie sighed, tucked her sneakered feet under her on the sofa, and looked at the wall beyond Adeline. A series of mauve watercolours—lilies, pansies, and coral-bells hung primly in turf-green frames.

"Why would you think that?" Adeline asked. She set down her tea, picked up a match, and lit the candle on the coffee table between them. The flame flickered, smoked, bent, and waivered before its shape gelled into a teardrop and stretched toward heaven.

Chorie inhaled. Cinnamon. "I think Gus is going to say I'm too emotionally unstable to be a fit mother."

"But you would argue the fact you're seeking help to deal with those issues shows you're in command of your life. You've established a support network." Adeline picked up her tea, leaned back in her chair, and wrapped both hands around the cup. She ran the steam beneath her nose and fixed her eyes on the candle flame.

"I suppose," Chorie said. "I'm so glad Gus didn't get Kryssie across the border. He lied to me, you know. He said he had an appointment, but he didn't. I think he believed if he showed up with a sick child they'd have no choice but to see her. The homecare nurse says they wouldn't have, though."

"Where is your daughter now?"

"She's in a foster home. I was told I could see her whenever I want so I've taken myself a pillow and blanket and I'm camping out on the floor in her room. I brought her the petite point her grandmother made her and hung it over her bed where she can see it. I'm trying to make it seem like home to her. I put her teddy bear and Barbie dolls on the window sill."

"You're a very good mother."

"Gus is a good father, too. It should never have come to this. We both love that child to bits. I so much wish we could love her together. Cry together...Love each other."

"It will work out. I know it will. It won't be long at all until you'll have Krystaline back in your living room."

"Do you know about...Schrödinger's cat?" Chorie asked hesitantly.

Adeline wrinkled her nose. "It sounds familiar."

"Quantum Physics. The Many Worlds Theory?"

"I have a basic idea of the concept, but don't ask me for the math!"

"Someone said it may not be just vivid dreams I'm having. I may be accessing another reality."

"Who said that?" Adeline demanded. She set her mug down with a bang and leaned toward Chorie.

"Just...someone."

"I think your 'someone' is bluffing you. I know enough about Quantum Physics to know the scientific principles operating at the quanta level don't translate into real life experiences! Chordelia, these are subatomic particles we're talking about. So tiny, they've never been seen, only theorized..."

"No, you're wrong," Chorie interrupted. "I saw a photo on the internet. They've very recently been able to capture a visual image of an electron."

"Well, either way, Newton's Laws, not Quantum laws, govern the observable universe."

"It was an educated person who told me this," Chorie persisted. "Actually, he's...a psychiatrist. He..."

"A psychiatrist told you that you're experiencing alternate realities?"

"Yes."

"I have a hard time believing that! It goes against psychiatric principles to reinforce a patient's delusions! Chordelia, what's happening here is that you're having trouble accepting your daughter's going to die. You're fantasizing it is otherwise, in order to deal with the possibility. Although that may be comforting for now, in the long run, if you don't eventually come to terms with reality, you're not going to be able to get through the grieving process."

Chorie felt the warm tickle of tears.

"I'm truly sorry," Adeline apologized softly. "It's not up to me to destroy your hope. In fact, it's also against psychiatric principles to argue with you about your delusions. What psychiatrist have you been seeing?"

"One in Seattle—in my other life. He was very real…"

"Chordelia, listen to yourself. Listen to what you're saying. He's part of the dream world you've made up…"

"No! He can't be! He told me about Schrödinger's cat and Everett's Many Worlds Theory. He gave me websites to check! How would I know about shit like that if he was a just a figment of my imagination?"

Adeline smiled at her wanly, a mixture of pity and understanding in her eyes. "It's okay. For now, I'll let you have your fantasy. But accept that's what it is, Chordelia. Just something warm and fuzzy for you to cling to when the anguish becomes too painful to bear."

CHAPTER 9

Chorie stood nervously before the heavy oak courtroom doors. At any moment, they were going to swing open. She was going to speak to the judge. She was going to get her daughter back. She felt a hand on her shoulder and turned.

"How are you doing?" Adeline whispered.

"Okay, I guess," Chorie said. "I can hardly wait for it to be over." Behind Adeline, in a shadowy corner not far down the hall, she could see Gus. He was speaking with a small man in an expensive suit. A shiny black briefcase, decked out with brilliant gold snaps and buttons, was propped on the marble tiles between them.

"I should have brought a lawyer, too," Chorie said.

"This is Family Court," Adeline said. "A lawyer's an unnecessary expense. The judge isn't looking at illegalities and points of law. He's not out to assign guilt or blame. He just needs to determine what's best for the child. You'll do fine."

The big doors opened and a man in a stiff uniform motioned the four of them in. Gus' lawyer smiled at her, as if they were friends, as she made her way with the others to the front row seats.

"My client's daughter," the lawyer began at the judge's request, "is seriously ill and needs immediate decisions made regarding her medical care."

"There's a dispute between the parents regarding appropriate medical care?" the judge queried.

"There should be no dispute," Chorie put in. "I'm following all medical advice we've been given." Tears welled up in her eyes and she glanced at Gus. He was stonefaced but she knew his heart was crying along with hers.

"There's nothing more that can be done for her," Chorie sobbed. "Just palliative care to make her comfortable during her last days. And I'm giving her that. Gus must accept this."

"Your Honour, as you can well understand, this is a very stressful time for both parents and my client in no way wishes to insinuate the mother is neglectful. But he has serious questions about her emotional stability and her hold on reality. He must be free to take over the parenting decisions."

"Likewise, your Honour," Chorie said. "I know Gus loves Krystaline and only wants the best for her. He doesn't want her die, but she's going to, sir. He wants to take her out of the country for experimental treatments that go against all medical advice we've been given. He mustn't be allowed to do that! Despite his best intentions, this is not what's best for our daughter. The treatment is extremely invasive, painful and totally unproven. Krystaline must be allowed to die peacefully. At home. With me beside her."

Gus' lawyer smiled at her sympathetically. "The mother is a little delusional. My client has no wish to take his very sick daughter out of the country."

"But he's already tried to!" Chorie protested. "He tricked me out of the house and took off with her in the motor home and…"

"Your Honour, the mother is extremely stressed. My client arranged an afternoon at the spa for her and took his daughter on a little outing. Little Kryssie was very comfortable, able to lie down and look out the windows. Gus had his mother along, who is a nurse, and he drove to his daughter's favourite park, where they shared good memories. There was no abduction planned…."

"But there was! He snuck off with her…."

"I don't think it's a requirement of good parenting that every little decision must be discussed. The father believed his wife was enjoying some badly needed time away from the stress of caring for the child…."

"That's a lie! It's all a lie! Gus," she said turning to stare into her husband's eyes. "Tell me this yourself with a straight face! Tell me those were your intentions!"

"Is there someone here," the judge asked, "who can speak to the mother's emotional state?"

"Adeline Simms, sir," her counsellor introduced, rising. "Psychologist. I've been counselling the mother for several months. She's very stressed and is becoming increasingly delusional…."

Chorie stared at Adeline. Her heart was thumping so loudly she was unable to hear the rest of the women's words. Adeline's lips were moving, her eyes were on the judge, she looked very far away. Unfamiliar.

"Is it your opinion," the judge's deep voice finally came through to her, "that these delusions are putting the child at risk?"

"I don't see any immediate risk, but it would be my advice that the mother not remain the primary caregiver…."

"I want a lawyer!" Chorie shouted. "I was told I didn't need one, but I obviously do. I demand these proceedings cease until I retain legal counsel!"

"Sir," Gus' lawyer objected, "due to the frailty of the child and need for immediate decisions surrounding her care, this matter must be resolved expeditiously."

"Let me get this straight," the judge said, setting his eyes on Chorie. "You disagree with what Ms. Simms has said about your mental state?"

"She's misinterpreting! I'm not delusional! I was merely telling her about some vivid dreams I've been having. I think the fact that, unlike Krystaline's father, I'm aware of my stress and seeking help and… building myself a support network…I need a lawyer."

"Are you saying you *don't* believe you're living in an alternate reality?"

"No, sir. I don't. I wouldn't even have thought of such a thing if a psychiatrist hadn't mentioned it to me."

"A psychiatrist mentioned it to you?"

"May I interrupt?" Adeline requested. "What may have started out as a comforting daydream about her daughter being well, has become increasingly real to my client. She believes one of her imagined characters in this other 'reality' is a psychiatrist who has given her secret information about Quantum Physics that verifies the reality of her imaginings. She…."

"Everett's Many Worlds Theory!" Chorie shouted. "It's not a secret! It's real! Scientists believe it! It's on the internet…in science magazines. It's the most important knowledge of the twenty-first century!"

"Ma'am, I'll honour your request to get legal counsel," the Judge said. "But due to the emergent nature of this case, I'll grant interim custody to the father. The child will remain accessible to the mother at all times, but visitations must be supervised."

"He mustn't take her out of the country!" Chorie insisted.

"Very well. I'll make that a condition of the custody order. Until this thing is settled, the child is to remain in the country."

"Remain in my home!"

"Sir, what living arrangements do you have in mind?" the judge asked Gus.

Gus looked at his shoes and coughed before meeting the judge's gaze. "As Krystaline requires special medical attention, I intended my mother to look after her and as my wife and mother don't get along well and as I have no desire to further stress Chorie by removing her from the family home, I intended sir, for Krystaline to live separately...."

"Are you moving her in with Deanna?" Chorie screamed. "That's what's happening, isn't it? You're setting up housekeeping with your secretary? You're cutting me out of your life! Taking my daughter from me! Gus, Kryssie's dying! She needs to be with her mother. She needs to be in her own home! She needs that, Gus! You know she does! She definitely doesn't need your mother! Gus! Look at me! Look at me!"

CHAPTER 10

"I don't believe you'd do this to me!" Chorie moaned.

"Do what to you?" Gus asked.

Chorie flashed open her eyes and laid her palm on her belly. She could almost feel the movements beneath her hand. It wouldn't be long before she'd need maternity clothes. She sucked in a breath. Lavender. "Sorry, I was just thinking."

"Thinking about what?"

"Well, just wondering…If we were to have a serious dispute about some aspect of raising Krystaline, something very important, how far would you go to overrule me?"

"Are you asking me whom I love more, my wife or my daughter?"

"Oh…I guess if you put it that way, the answer is obvious."

"That wasn't an answer, Chorie; it was a question. Why are you assuming the obvious answer was to your question?"

"Well, if you're any kind of a parent, of course the child will come first over anything or anybody."

"I don't know," Gus said thoughtfully. "Not necessarily. Although one can never know for sure how one will react, I could see myself deferring to your judgement. After all, you've done an excellent job so far as a mother. I'd likely respect your decision."

"Even if you thought my decision was putting her in danger?"

"I can't see you making decision that would endanger her."

"Well, something like…Let's say she's sick, perhaps dying, and you want to sign her up from some kind of experimental medical treatment as a last resort and I don't…"

"Chorie, are you still obsessing over your nightmare about Krystaline dying?"

"No," Chorie said quickly. "No. But, it just got me thinking about things like this. I'm just using it as an example. To stimulate discussion between us. Don't you think something like that would be really hard to negotiate through?"

"Undoubtedly. Just the fact the child is dying, would be hard. But I wish you wouldn't talk about shit like this. What's the point? Can't we discuss realistic parenting issues? Less morbid ones?"

"I'm sorry. You're right."

"Have you run out of the pills that Seattle doctor prescribed?"

"Actually, he didn't prescribe any, which is probably good considering I'm pregnant. I'm leery of all medications."

"Well, he seemed to calm you down somehow. What did he do?"

"He talked to me about Schrödinger's cat. Do you know about the quantum cat?"

"Yeah," Gus chuckled. "I know about the cat. I actually took several physics courses at university."

"You know, too, then about the Many World's Theory?"

"Fascinating, isn't it?"

"Do you think it's true?"

"Seems to be. Mathematically and experimentally, everything leads to that conclusion. You know, Schrödinger initially hypothesized the cat to refute the underlying tenets of Quantum Physics—to show its absurdity. Then Everett stepped in with his theory, which he thought solved the paradox. Of course, his theory is perhaps even more absurd than Schrödinger's cat."

"So you don't think there are multiple universes?"

"There probably are, it's their relevancy I can't fathom. Other than an explanation for Quantum behaviour, it seems a useless idea. I mean, who cares? We can't exchange any type of information between the realities. If you can't see something, taste it, feel it, measure it, detect it, affect it, in what sense is it real?"

"Oh. So you think many worlds exist, but no one can ever explore them?"

"That's what the science says."

"That's not what the doctor said," Chorie muttered.

"What did the doctor say?"

"He said my dream may actually be an alternate realty. He says I may somehow be tapping into one of Everett's Many Worlds."

"He didn't say that! Are you serious? He said that?"

Chorie nodded.

"I'm sorry," Gus said. "He came highly recommended. No one said anything about him being crazy. Look, Chorie, I'll set you up with a local doctor. I'll make sure this time I pick a sane shrink."

"No, actually I kind of liked the Seattle guy. He said if I kept having problems, I could come back and he'd help me. I'd like to go see him again, Gus."

"Mommy! Mom! Mom!" Krystaline called from the back entry.

"Don't yell at me, Kryssie! If you want to talk, come into the kitchen!"

"Mom, I just want to know if you washed my soccer jersey!"

"It's hanging on the drying rack on the balcony. Your socks, too!"

"I'm going to have to miss her game again this evening," Gus said.

"Why?"

"I've got to go back to the office. I thought we had a winner with Stephen, but it turns out he's not quite as good as he bragged himself up to be. I have to straighten out his errors before tomorrow's meeting. I don't mind someone making mistakes, but when they blame everybody and everything else instead of taking responsibility...I think that man's on his way out!"

CHAPTER 11

"I'd like you to reconsider," Strongberg, Chops, & Lamb, Barristers and Solicitors said. Chorie had pulled the law firm's name off the internet and had no idea which of the trio had reluctantly agreed to meet her.

"Reconsider?" Chorie asked. She'd unluckily chosen probably the most pompous lawyer in Alberta. He had a gold pen that was likely real gold. A million certificates, awards, and photos of celebrities shaking his hand covered the wall behind him. His woolly grey eyebrows, which were perpetually raised, seemed to be holding his nose in the air.

"Custody isn't all it's made out to be," he continued. "You must be exhausted from looking after your daughter for so long. It could be a blessing that someone else steps in."

Chorie caught sight of his nameplate peaking around the files that cluttered his desk. 'Tessman Strongberg, Esq.', in some Gothic script, etched into a brass plate mounted on a chunk of rich mahogany.

Chorie sniffed. She might have been able to catch its soft scent if the tinny odour of death wasn't coating her nostrils.

"Do you have children?" Chorie asked.

"No. No, I don't."

"Is there someone else available who does have children?"

"I was trying to be gentle," he said. "Put more bluntly, you don't have a chance in hell of regaining custody."

"Why not?"

"Because you're crazy."

"I'm not crazy!"

"You find a psychiatrist to back you on that and I'll reconsider. In the meanwhile, take advantage of your visiting rights. Be with the child as often as you like. I give you that advice free of charge."

"My rights?" Chorie leaned forward in her chair, put her fists on his desk, and slowly rose. "My husband is planning to move in with his secretary and I have the right to join them in their love nest, does that seem adequate 'rights' to you?"

She heard her voice rise, tremble, and bounce off the walls. She knew it she was being inappropriate, but she couldn't stop.

"I want to be with my daughter, day and night. Hear every whimper. Dry every tear. I want to cool her fevered forehead. Swab glycerine on her cracked tongue. I want to wipe the vomit from her lips. I want to sing her lullabies. I want to monitor her IV. I want to be holding her hand when she passes from this world. And, Mr. Strongberg…" She leaned so far into him he was compelled to tip back his chair. "I sure as fuck don't want to be doing it in Deanna's spare bedroom!"

She inched closer and locked her eyes on his. She felt her breasts brush the folder of papers before him.

"Ma'am," he said, finally shaking free of her gaze. "Please, sit. Please." Chorie kept her eyes on his face as she slowly slumped into her chair.

"Ma'am, like I said, if you can get someone to vouch for your sanity. In the meantime, I suggest you continue with your counselling…"

"Continue with my counselling?" Chorie interrupted. "My counsellor testified against me! I'd like to sue her for breach of confidentiality! She had no right to reveal the content of our sessions…"

"When a child is at risk, she not only has a right to, but has a legal and moral obligation to."

"She said the child wasn't at risk! She said I was no danger…"

"She was just being kind! If it were my child, I'd sure as hell be wondering who was looking after her while you were out meandering in alternate universes!"

"You don't understand the true nature of time, do you? It's not as if I divide my time between lives. Time is not linear; it's multi-dimensional. Simultaneous, in a way. I'm not absent from one life while pursuing the other…"

"Listen!" Strongberg interrupted loudly. "Listen! This is irrelevant to the case! There is no way I'm arguing quantum physics or the nature of time before a judge in a court of law!" He picked up his pen, pulled his chair forward, and lowered his voice. "Ma'am, even if I were to agree to do that for you, it sure as hell wouldn't get you custody!"

Chorie leaned back in her chair and squeezed shut her eyes.

"I'm sorry. I truly am. But there is just no way I can take on this case."

Chorie knew she was supposed to leave. Get up and walk out. But she couldn't. She couldn't move. She couldn't open her eyes or her mouth.

Perhaps because she had nowhere to go and never would. Krystaline would die and Gus would be with Deanna. And she'd be somewhere, nowhere, traversing realities. Crazy. In an institution."

Strongberg coughed. She heard leather squeak as he shifted in his chair. In the distance, behind his thick dark mahogany door, a phone softly jangled.

"When I refuse a case, the firm refuses the case," the lawyer finally said.

She wondered what would happen if she didn't leave; if she just sat here. Would he call in the cops? Would they arrest her for trespassing, lock her up? Transfer her in shackles to the insane asylum? Would Strongberg simply sit and stare at her and charge her by the hour?

"Ma'am?"

She had to get out of this reality. She had to hunt down the Seattle doctor, get his help. She definitely could not relax into the experience.

"Ma'am, are you all right?"

She couldn't answer. Couldn't nod. Couldn't cry.

"Ma'am? Ma'am! Are you in another world?"

CHAPTER 12

"We should surprise Daddy and stop by his office. We can tell him you won 'player of the game'," Chorie said. She kicked off her heels, threw them into the back seat, and started the car. "Krystaline, do up your seatbelt." Chorie pulled down her visor and looked in the vanity mirror. Summer sun was harsh on the skin. She freshened her lipstick and rubbed some lavender lotion over her cheeks before shifting into gear.

"And I scored two goals! He'll like that!" Krystaline said.

Chorie turned onto the street and tossed Krystaline her cell phone. "Here. Call home and make sure he hasn't already left the office."

Krystaline dialled then tossed the phone onto the dash. "There's no answer, just the voice message."

Chorie pulled into the Triple G Architects parking lot. "Yeah, he's still at work," Chorie said. "There's his truck." She wondered who owned the only other vehicle in the lot—a little red Mazda. It looked like a woman's car. Perhaps, a secretary's car. Parked right beside Gus' Avalanche.

The outer door of the office complex was locked—which wasn't so unusual, she supposed. It was after hours. If there was no one at the reception desk, Gus wouldn't want people wandering in unnoticed. She rummaged in her purse for the key.

She caught the smell of a scented candle as she pushed open the door. There was music playing—not a radio but a high-definition quality CD. Classical. Romantic. She heard voices. A giggle.

"Wait here, Krystaline. I'll make sure he's not in a meeting or something."

Or something…Her heart pounded as she slithered down the unlit hall toward his office. It couldn't be. She'd just found out they were pregnant. It's what he wanted. He was a family man. A wonderful father. A husband.

The music got louder. The voices, too. The giggle. The scent of an evening in Paris. His door was slightly ajar. She pushed it open.

"Krystaline won player of the game," she said loudly. Gus jumped to his feet and tugged at his trousers. "She scored two goals."

Deanna lay half-naked on the lounger. A vixen smile on her face. She ran her ruby nails over the red lace of her bra, down the curve of her waist. She tucked her pinkie under the band of her crimson panties.

"When you're done here, Gus," Chorie said. "Come home and we'll talk about it." She returned Deanna's smile with one of her own before walking out.

"He is in a meeting, Krystaline," she said, draping her arm over her daughter's shoulder and hustling her out the exit. "You'll have to wait until he gets home to tell him."

"What's the matter, Mommy?"

"Nothing's the matter," Chorie said, striding across the parking lot pavement.

"Is something wrong with Daddy?"

"Nothing's wrong, dear. Get in the car. I guess I'm just upset that he's too busy for us. I shouldn't be. It's not his fault he has to work so hard. And it's his hard work that buys us all the good stuff..." She knew she was prattling, but she couldn't stop. It was as though she were rehearsing for that moment in time when she'd have to explain the divorce to her daughter.

"He works very, very, hard. Fasten your seatbelt," she continued. "Although I know he'd much rather have been with you at soccer, he really has no choice. He would have loved to have seen you play tonight; I know he would have..."

And someday she'd be saying, *Daddy won't be going with you to the soccer tournament in Hinton, because that's the weekend it's my turn to have you. He loves you, though. It's not your fault. We both love you. He's a good father. He loves you...He loves the baby...He loves...*

"He's tried to hire someone to help him so he doesn't have to put in such long hours, but it didn't work out. The man made mistakes and Daddy has to fix them. It takes a lot of time to fix mistakes. Especially someone else's mistakes. So he had to do all that, plus all his own work. I'm sure he'll be home soon and you can tell him about your game..."

When you go to Daddy's next weekend, you can tell him about your game...

"If it gets too late, after bedtime, I'll make sure he peaks in on you and gives you a kiss. If you're still awake, you can talk to him..."

You can talk to Daddy on the phone. Wish him goodnight...

CHAPTER 13

"I'm so sorry," Gus said, walking slowly toward her. He stopped at the entry to the kitchen. "There's nothing I can say to make this any better, is there?"

Chorie looked up at him, shook her head 'no', and then stared back down at her herbal tea. The baby in her tummy somersaulted.

"Is Krystaline in bed?"

"She's asleep."

"I don't know what to say." Gus took a tentative step toward her.

"I suppose you'll be using Lanktin for the divorce," Chorie said. "I'll have to find myself a different lawyer."

"Can't we talk about it?" Gus pleaded.

"What's there to talk about?"

"I want to say all the usual things…It was a mistake. It just happened…It meant nothing…."

"I don't want to be married to a man to whom sex means nothing."

Gus closed his eyes and nodded. He jammed his hands in his pockets. Looked down at his shoes and then up to the ceiling.

"Don't worry about the baby," Chorie said. "I'll book an abortion tomorrow. No need to screw up the lives of two children."

"Chorie!" he protested, walking swiftly toward her. "No! No! Don't. Don't do that. Talk to me, please. Let's talk about it first, before you decide anything."

"Go ahead. Talk."

"I want to tell you all my excuses," he said, settling in across the table from her. "You probably don't want to hear them, though, do you?"

Chorie shrugged. "You're the one who wants to talk. If it's excuses you want to talk about…go for it."

"Chorie." He sighed. Tears streamed from the corners of his eyes, cascaded over his defined cheekbones, washed over his smooth, dark, skin. Dripped onto his collar. "I've just been so stressed lately. I've tried to keep it from you because I know you're stressed yourself. And pregnant and everything. But it's bad at work. Pressure. And then I come home and you carry on these bizarre conversations. Half the time it seems like you're in another world. I know it sounds stupid, but I've been feeling so lonely. So...." He sniffled, wiped at his nose and his eyes, and rose to get a tissue. He kept his back to her. His shoulders were shaking violently.

"I see," Chorie said.

"I didn't want to hurt you. I didn't want to hurt Krystaline. Please don't just end everything. Don't get rid of the baby. I know I don't have any right to ask you for any of this...I know that. But, please. Please give me a chance to make this right."

"Another world," Chorie whispered.

"You just seemed so distant. Preoccupied...

"Gus, this wasn't supposed to happen in this world. In my other world it was happening, but not in this world. We were happy in this world. Kryssie wasn't dying! Stephen was working out okay. I was pregnant, and happy. And you cared about my feelings." She turned and flung her teacup into the sink. "This wasn't supposed to happen!"

"Do you want me to leave?" he asked; his back still to her.

"I don't know. I don't know anything!" She rose, put her hands on the counter, and stared into the sink. Chards of white china. A broken cup. A broken heart. Crazy. Going crazy.

"I know you didn't need this right now," he said. She could tell from his voice he'd turned toward her. She heard his footsteps approach. Could feel the heat of his body behind her and hear the sound of his breathing. "Can you ever forgive me?"

"I don't know."

"If it helps any, things never got any farther than what you saw tonight."

"That doesn't help."

"I'll leave," he said. "I'll phone you from the motel. Let you know where I am."

She heard him retreating. Slowly. Hesitantly.

"Is there anything you'd like me to do?" he asked from a few feet behind her.

"Don't leave. Stay with your daughter. Go on your computer and book me a flight to Seattle."

"Sure," he said. She watched him slowly walk toward his den. He stopped. Turned to her. His eyes red. His cheeks wet. "A return flight?"

"Just one way, for now. And book me into the hotel we stayed at last time. Make me an appointment with that Seattle psychiatrist, Doctor Penny."

"Sure," he said. He dropped his head. "Are you coming back? I kind of have to know. For Krystaline. If I have to make arrangements…with work and sitters and stuff."

"I don't know if I'm coming back. Make whatever arrangements you want to."

CHAPTER 14

Anger finally overcame her self-pity and Chorie flashed open her eyes. She smelled it on herself—tin and nickel for death and steel for strength.

"Yes, Mr. Strongberg," she hissed. "I'm in another world! If you'd been listening to me, you'd realize that! You'd also realize that being in another world doesn't preclude me from being in this world! In fact," she said, grabbing her purse and rising, "in my other world I'm on my way to a psychiatrist who believes I'm sane!" She strode to the door and flung it open.

"Bring back a note from him vouching for that!" Strongberg snickered.

She slammed the door behind her.

If only it were that easy! Dr. Penny probably didn't even exist in this reality, at least not as a Seattle psychiatrist. And she didn't exactly exist in his reality, either. Hell, in his world she was pregnant. Kryssie wasn't sick. And Gus was philandering because she was being driven crazy by the mess in this life.

As she flung open the door to the street, she caught a whiff of autumn. The September sun was trying to hold onto summer. It was shining as bright as it could, a full gold disk in the azure sky. But it was no match for the north wind. Not today.

She hugged her sweater tighter and walked across the lot to her car. In the boulevard, red berries decked out the mountain ash. Crisp yellow leaves were falling from the aspen and shuffling across the green grass. She inhaled deeply. She loved autumn. Always had. The smells. The colours. The first day of school. Opening a pristine box of crayons. Turning back the cover of brand new reader and hearing the crinkle run down its spine. The smell of fresh ink.

There would be no first day of school for Krystaline this year. There would never be another first day of school. She glanced up at a small flock of honking Canada geese. They were getting ready to fly south; an arduous trip with warm sunshine at its end.

It would not be long before Krystaline, too, made her journey. Like the geese, she would not be here for Christmas.

Chorie hit the remote unlock and crawled into her car. She fastened her seatbelt, turned the key. She was never again going to leave her daughter's side. She was going to be there, holding her hand, when Krystaline left on her journey.

She was going to ignore Deanna, Gus, the mother-in-law, Adeline, Strongberg because…it was the only way she could make that happen.

CHAPTER 15

"Doctor Penny!" Chorie said, rushing into his office. In a desperate attempt to avoid his hypnotic gaze, she glued her eyes to the file on his desk. The scent of lavender wafted up from her cleavage. "I'm not relaxing into this experience! Make it go away!"

"Have a seat," he instructed in his deep, melodic voice. It was eerie how quickly his words dissipated into the plush surroundings.

She reluctantly turned from him and sank into the recliner. In the subdued lighting, amidst the dark colours, she felt so vulnerable. What if the doctor was insane, as Gus had suggested? She cast her eyes to the thick dark carpet. The trail of her footprints was clearly visible in the pile.

"This isn't something to be taken lightly," he intoned.

"I'm taking nothing lightly."

"What is it you want me to make disappear?"

"One of my lives," Chorie said. "A single life is hard enough. Two, is impossible."

"Did you do the research I assigned you?"

Chorie nodded. "It didn't help."

"If you'd done it properly, you'd understand I can't make a life disappear! Whatever can possibly happen; does happen. It's a fundamental scientific principle. I can't change that any more than I can vanquish gravity!"

"You told me you could help me," Chorie moaned.

"I can. I'll set you up with a support group. You can learn some of the techniques others use to manage the phenomenon."

"No! I don't want to manage this! In one life I've lost custody of my dying daughter because I've been judged insane and in the other I'm losing my husband because he senses I'm lost between worlds, in a place he can't come."

"I'll do nothing more for you until you at least try. Many have become quite successful at isolating their emotional responses within the appropriate reality."

"If I wasn't going through such an intensely emotional time, perhaps

I'd consider it. But, Doctor, my daughter is dying! I've lost custody of her! My husband is having an affair with his secretary and their love nest is the only place I can be with my daughter—with his pathetic mother present! How do I isolate all that?"

"You must consider it."

"Why?"

"What is it you imagine you want me to do for you?"

"Make it go away!"

"Make what go away?"

"Make one of my lives go away!"

"Which one?"

"The one where my daughter's dying, of course!"

"Your daughter is going to die, regardless of what I do, because whatever can possibly happen, will happen. Are you saying you want to forego the intense experience of being with her when she does?"

Chorie thought of her vow never to leave her daughter's side. To be with her until the end. To be holding her hand when she took her last breath.

"Of course," the doctor chuckled, "you will be there, no matter what I do."

"What are you saying? Do I or don't I have the choice of which life I give up?"

"No. You don't."

"But you asked!"

"I'm only in this particular reality with you and therefore can only manipulate the body and brain you present in this reality. You therefore must be certain you're willing to give up the other reality and proceed in this one. You and your other world will continue, but you will lose all awareness of it."

He began scribbling furiously. "The support group is actually meeting tonight. Here are the particulars." He ripped off his page of notes and held it out to her.

She stood and reached for the paper. He caught her eyes and held them. They were mystical eyes; dark. She struggled against their pull, undecided if their magnetic blackness was powered by a soul or the absence of one.

"Do yourself a favour," he said. "Take your time with your decision."

CHAPTER 16

It was obvious to Chorie from the overly enthusiastic but short-lived greeting from the support group that people were more intent on talking than on listening. Side conversations escalated in number and volume as the room filled. At the centre of the turmoil was a thin man, barely out of adolescence, with four rings in his nose and three in each ear. He flitted from person to person, his arms waving as his tongue told stories. He punctuated each sentence with a feminine, but loud, giggle.

"I have to tell you this! I just have to tell you this!" he exclaimed as the dozen people in the room began choosing chairs around the circle.

"Casey," a soft-spoken, grey-haired gentleman suggested to him. "Let everyone first take their seats, perhaps." The man was tall, muscular, and well tanned. He was probably the oldest in the room.

"Sit! Sit!" Casey began ordering, grabbing people's shoulders, and steering them toward chairs. "I've got to tell you this! This is amazing!

He danced in the middle of the circle until everyone was sitting. "I went back in time to the age of dinosaurs," he enthused. "No, don't laugh! It's the true nature of time. If only scientists would consider that when they're trying to get everything to fit into a linear scale of evolution. Man and dinosaur did exist together, at least in one world. Get this! Get this! There were fire-breathing dragons! The brontosaurs produced a lot of methane from their vegetative diet and when they got frightened, they'd clash their teeth, producing sparks that ignited their methane belches! Fire-breathing dragons are not just a myth. They were very real. Very, very, real! And people saw them!"

"That's so cool, Casey," a young woman said. She dipped her head and looked up at him through her lashes. "We can learn so much about our past from these experiences. I finally, finally, met Cleopatra! She's as beautiful as legend has it. And I found out the pyramids weren't constructed by a massive labour force dragging rocks down from the mountain and hauling them up the sides of the edifice. The ancients actually knew how to make concrete! Those stone blocks were poured in place, which makes a lot of sense. It explains why there's no chisel or hammer marks on the stones."

The older man who'd spoke to Casey at the beginning rose and began walking to the back of the room. "Coffee?" he mouthed, catching Chorie's eye.

Chorie slithered from her seat unnoticed and followed him to the coffee urn and donuts laid out in the back. "I can't compete with those stories," she whispered.

"Neither can I," the man said, rolling his eyes in distain. "Sugar?" he asked motioning to a cup of coffee he'd poured.

"Sure."

He dropped in a cube and passed it to her. "This was once a useful group—until the media got hold of it. Now every wacko on the continent shows up!" He sighed and raised his coffee to his lips.

"My name's Chorie."

"Daniel." He took a sip and nodded to the door. "I expect at any moment, Shirley McLain will walk in."

"Perhaps we're just as wacko as the rest?" Chorie offered.

"Perhaps." Daniel pulled a newspaper clipping from his breast pocket. "Maybe the good doctor is, too. Did you see the articles they did on Doctor Penny and his groups?"

Chorie shook her head. "I'm not from here. I'm from Canada."

"Well, this is the result," he said handing her the clipping. "The Association of Psychiatrists is investigating him for unprofessional conduct. They say it is against their code of ethics to reinforce a patient's delusions. He has a disciplinary hearing in two days. He's also being accused of performing unproven surgical intervention when he isn't qualified to perform even proven surgery."

"He performs surgery?" Chorie asked, scanning the article.

"It's what he does if you insist on getting rid of one of your lives. He's theorized that a deep part of the brain is acting as an antenna, so to speak, and picking up signals from other worlds. He believes this part of the brain is normally where intuition, creative thinking, instinctive behaviour, and perhaps dreaming, originate. Something either in the genetic makeup of certain individuals or in their environments stimulates that part excessively. He's recorded the hyperactivity on MRI's. He zaps that part of the brain to deaden the nerves that are firing excessively."

"Oh," Chorie said, handing him back the paper. "I was hoping for some kind of pill to swallow."

"I take it you're seriously considering getting rid of one of your worlds?"

"Not get rid of it," Chorie said, smiling up at him. "Everything that could possibly happen—does. I just want to get rid of my access to it. Everyone in both my worlds thinks I'm crazy. I can't carry on. What about you?"

"In one of my lives I'm living with my high school sweetheart, having never met my wife. Both women keep accusing me of cheating. Women's intuition, I guess."

"Do you want to get rid of one of the women?"

"I don't know. My wife and I have children. A happy and fulfilling life."

"Does the sweetheart have to go?"

"That would be my choice. It can't be, though. Doctor Penny is with me in the high school sweetheart reality. He can only block out the wife... and children...I can't fathom a life without my son and daughter. Either that, or he can kill me in this world and let me live on in the other."

"Kill you? Murder?" Chorie gasped.

"Just in this world," Daniel said. "I believe I'd be ever so grateful, as would my wife. It is something I've considered."

Chorie remembered searching the doctor's dark, powerful eyes for a soul. How was it he'd convinced Daniel he ought to be murdered? Dr. Penny had to be evil. Insane. He was being chastised and ostracised by his peers. He was simply sucking in the vulnerable and sucking in the dollars. She was a fool to be here.

The baby in her belly kicked. She set down her coffee and lay her hand on her tummy.

"When's junior due?" Daniel asked.

She turned from him. "Some time around Christmas," she murmured, making her way past the circle of chairs to the exit.

CHAPTER 17

Chorie had surreptitiously made herself a copy of the key to Deanna's apartment and after once more deeply inhaling the autumn scents, she quietly let herself in.

The nickel-finished light fixtures, doorknobs, and hinges were the cold visual equivalent to the smell of death permeating the air. The place sported the modern look, barren of all things extraneous. The furniture, vases, drapes, and murals were a composition of vertical lines and sharp edges.

It was obvious a man didn't live here, or at least hadn't lived here for very long. There was nothing out of place. No tie on the railing, no jacket on the chair, no briefcase on the table.

It was such a sterile place for a child to die.

Chorie tiptoed past the living room where Lila was sitting, a book open on her lap, her head thrown back, and her mouth open— snoring.

"Mommy? Where were you?" Krystaline moaned.

"You were sleeping so I stepped out for a moment. I'm back now and I won't leave again."

"Take me home, please."

"You ask Daddy when he comes."

"He said you could take me home."

"Well, if he said that, then I guess you have something to look forward to."

"Let's not wait for him."

"We should wait for him. We need his help to carry you, sweetheart. Just have a little sleep and he'll be here when you wake up."

"Ah," Deanna interrupted from the doorway. "I thought I heard voices." She stuck her hands, except for her thumbs, in the front pockets of her jeans and leaned against the door-frame. "Gus asked me to talk to you. Come with me to the kitchen."

"I'm not leaving my daughter."

"Perhaps if you knew what I was going to say, you'd change your mind about wanting your daughter to hear it."

"If that's the case, perhaps you shouldn't say it."

"Have you found yourself a lawyer yet?"

"That's not you business."

"I'm asking on behalf of Gus."

"Gus can ask on behalf of himself. I'm not discussing this with you, Deanna."

"Due to the emergent nature of this situation, Gus will be asking for an immediate review of the custody order. His lawyer says if you're refusing to go to counselling, there should be nothing standing in Gus' way of getting full custody and limiting your visiting."

Chorie kicked off her sneakers and snuggled onto the bed beside Krystaline. She gently ran her fingertips over her daughter's hot, dry cheek. "Deanna, I said I'm not discussing this with you."

"I can't believe you're doing this to you own daughter! If she were my child, I'd be doing everything possible to save her life."

Chorie fluffed her pillow and closed her eyes. "Please leave."

"Gus says you never wanted children? Perhaps that's behind your decisions?"

"Shush. You're keeping the child awake."

"You do realize he will be taking her to the Seattle clinic. One way or another."

Chorie heard the door squeak closed.

"Daddy doesn't want me to die. I'm trying not to," Krystaline whispered.

"We're both going to miss you so very much, but you do what you have to, Kryssie."

"But…," she said, struggling to turn her head. She stared into Chorie's face. "If I die, he'll be mad at you!"

"Don't worry about that, sweetheart. Some people find it very hard to be sad, so instead, they get angry. I'll know that's what it is. I'll help him learn how to be sad."

"I don't like Deanna. I want to go home!"

"Shush, sweets. Close your eyes and sleep for a bit." She wrapped her fingers around Krystaline's. "I won't leave this time."

CHAPTER 18

"You're home!" Gus said. The relief on his face was obvious, though she could tell he was trying to curb it. He scanned her face.

"Yes, I'm home." Chorie set her suitcase down and pulled off her gloves. She wiped at the snow melting down her nose. She caught the scent—lavender lotion, the promise of spring.

"And…?"

"And…" Chorie stared at her husband. He was so worried. Distraught. No one in the whole world cared for her like he did. He was the closest she could come to finding someone who understood her. Unbidden tears filled her eyes. "And I'm sorry, Gus. I've come back more mixed up than when I left."

She began to sob. He stepped toward her and pulled her gently to his chest. She buried her head in the soft flannel of his shirt. She heard his familiar heartbeat, felt his strong arms wrap tightly around her. She smelled the rain in his aftershave.

"It's me who ought to be sorry, darling," he whispered. "And I am."

"I wanted to come back sane for you," she said. "It didn't happen. I'm so sorry."

"Please don't say you're sorry! You've done nothing wrong. It was me…"

"I don't want you to leave me. But I'm scared you will if I can't get my act together."

"Honey! Honey! It's okay. Don't cry. I'm not intending on leaving you. Unless that's what you want, baby. I'm here for you. I promise."

"Gus," Chorie sobbed. "I need help."

"I know. I know." He rested his head on her curls, pulled her tighter, and rocked gently. "I know. And I should've been helping."

"It shouldn't be all about me. You've got your own problems, too. I know that. I should've been there for you. I want to be there for you."

"Come," he said, drawing back and taking her hand. "Let's sit and talk."

She followed him into the kitchen and took a seat as he plugged in the kettle. He pulled two teabags from the canister. "Is Camomile tea okay?"

"My favourite," Chorie said, wiping the tears from her cheeks.

"I promised I'd find you another psychiatrist, and I didn't."

"I think I told you I didn't want one. But, Gus, Doctor Penny is… weird. He's under investigation. He said he could help me, but—"

"He didn't do something bad to you, did he? He didn't do something…."

"No, not like that. No. I'm mostly upset because of what he wasn't able to do, not something he did."

"Okay. That's good." The kettle began whistling and Gus poured a bit of boiling water into each cup, swilled it around, and emptied the cups into the sink. He dropped a teabag in each mug. "What's he under investigation for?"

"Unethical conduct or something." Gus poured in the water. His actions were so familiar, so comforting. "His treatments are being criticized as unorthodox and unproven. I think he's crazier than I am."

"We'll find you someone new."

"How's Krystaline? Is she in bed?"

"She missed you lots. Yeah, I tucked her in an hour ago. She took a hit in soccer and twisted her knee. She's upset about being sidelined. She's a good little soccer player. Loves the sport."

"Is she hurt badly?"

"She'll be back in time to sign up for indoor soccer." Gus set their tea on the table, caught her eyes briefly, and then took the chair opposite the table from her. "Was your flight okay?"

Chorie twisted the cup to line up her fingers with the handle. Small talk. She smiled wanly. "I didn't lose my luggage."

"Where do you want to go from here?" Gus asked quietly.

"I don't know."

"It was wrong of me to blame you for what happened. I just wanted to—"

"It's okay," Chorie interrupted. Men liked to have reasons. "It takes two to make a marriage work, and two to rip it apart."

"Now that you're back," Gus said, shuffling his cup between his hands, "do you want me to leave? Move out?"

"No. I don't want to be alone, Gus. Let's try to make our marriage work."

CHAPTER 19

"Have I met you somewhere before?" the doctor asked, as she hustled Chorie into her office. "You look so familiar."

"Perhaps in another life," Chorie offered.

The doctor giggled. "No, seriously." She motioned Chorie to sit. Korean watercolours of pagodas, rivers, and rocks hung behind the doctor's desk. A small candle flickered beside the tape recorder on the teak coffee table between Chorie and the desk, its scent mingling with Chorie's perfume. Cinnamon and lavender—an odd combination.

Dr. Taylor drew a chair beside Chorie and leaned toward her. "You look so familiar," she repeated.

Chorie glanced at the certificate on the wall. *Dr. A. Taylor, Psychiatrist.* "Is your first name Adeline?" she asked.

"Yes. Yes it is."

"Did you once intend on being a psychologist rather than a psychiatrist?"

"You *do* know me from somewhere!"

"Yeah," Chorie sighed. "From another life. I don't think this is going to work."

"If I know you from outside my professional capacity and this is making you uncomfortable, it's certainly your right to seek out a different doctor."

"In my other life, your testimony caused me to lose custody of my daughter."

The doctor furrowed her brow, bent forward, and hit the record button on the tape machine. "I'm recording our session as…"

"Because you find taking notes interferes with the flow of the conversation."

"Exactly," the doctor said, slowly settling back into her chair.

"You told me that, too, in my other life."

"Your other life?"

"Since in that other life, you told me I created this life for comfort, perhaps in this life you'd like to explain why I created an imaginary world in which my daughter is dying?"

"This other life that you talk about, what's it like?"

"My daughter is sick, in pain, dying. I'm deemed crazy, have lost custody. My husband's fooling around with his secretary—threatening to take Krystaline to Seattle for invasive experimental treatment. That's what it's like."

"And this life?"

"My daughter's fine. I'm here because my other life is driving me insane and driving my husband into his secretary's bed."

"So, there are similarities between the two 'lives'?"

"Of course there are! I'm in both of them! You're in both of them! Gus, Krystaline, and Deanna are in both of them!"

"Which life do you prefer?"

Chorie rested her elbows on her knees, cradle her head in her hands, and stared at the doctor. "Do you not find that an inane question?"

"It's not a strange question. Some people thrive on excitement—tragedy. If they find their lives a trifle boring and predictable, they may create fantasies to compensate."

"If I wanted to create a fantasy, I'd make damned sure it involved a million dollars and Tom Cruise!"

"Tom Cruise? Does that reflect problems with your marriage?"

"Fuck!" Chorie muttered. She settled back in her chair and crossed her arms. "No, it reflects fantasy. If you think Tom Cruise would screw up my marriage, imagine what a dying child, a custody battle, a sexy secretary, and emotional baggage from two lives is doing—in both lives!"

"Which life seems the most real?"

"I don't know. My focus switches between them. Sometimes one, sometimes the other. When I first became aware of the problem, I was focused in the dying-daughter life and it seems that life is the most overwhelming. I more often confuse that reality with this one, than vice versa. Although, that isn't the life I'd choose…if given the choice."

"You'd want this life, the one you're in now?"

"This is the much better life! It would be perfect if I wasn't having this other life screwing me over."

"Perfect?"

"Compared to a dying daughter, yeah, perfect."

"I see. You said in this life your daughter is healthy?"

"Other than a gimped knee from soccer, yes. Healthy and happy. Always has been."

"And your marriage?"

"Suffering from the emotional trauma's in the other life."

"You blame your marriage problems on this 'other life'?"

"My husband does, too. He says he finds me distant, as if I'm in another world."

"Do you know of any reason why you would want this other life?"

"I don't want the other life! I want it to go away."

"Why won't it?"

"Schrödinger's cat," Chorie muttered.

"Pardon?"

"Someone suggested I'm accessing another reality, one of Everett's Many Worlds."

"Do you think that's what's happening?"

"Be damned if I know." Chorie squeezed her eyes shut. "Whatever it is, I just wish it would stop."

"Although to you it may seem like you're accessing another reality, I don't believe you are. Sometimes our brain chemistry gets out of whack and screws up our perceptions, our emotions, our memories. We could try a psychotropic drug to get that chemistry working properly again."

"A psychotropic drug? Like for schizophrenia?"

"I detect an element of depression along with your delusions. There are specific drugs that can help with both."

"I'm pregnant, though."

"Ah, yes. Right. When is baby due?"

"In a couple of months. Around Christmas."

"Are you happy with the pregnancy?"

"In my other life I don't want children. In this one, I'm quite happy with the prospect of a second child."

"Ah, I see. There's ambivalence toward motherhood, is there?"

"Only in the total picture. I'm quite firm in my desires in each of my lives."

"I see. There are some pills available that aren't too risky—especially at this late stage in the pregnancy, but it's up to you. Would you like to delay taking medication until after the baby is born? Until then, we could do some intensive therapy sessions."

"You think it's a problem with my brain chemistry?"

"I think you'll be quite happy with the results of medication."

"You don't think my other life is real? It's just a hallucination?"

"I'm not disputing the fact it seems real to you. Delusions can be defined as something that appears real to one person, but isn't perceived by those around them."

"My other life is perceived by those around me!" Chorie protested. "It's quite real. Why do you think I look familiar to you? How else could I have known your first name?"

"If it's your wish to abandon this other life, I'm quite sure the proper medication will do that for you."

CHAPTER 20

"You'll have to leave," Gus said from the bedroom door. He thumped a sheaf of papers against his palm. They were parchment-coloured legal-sized papers, like those which sported official seals—with lions and Latin that one could feel with one's fingers. Like papers signed by lawyers' and judges'. "The custody order has been revised."

"Gus," Chorie moaned, snuggling up closer to Krystaline. The rose lotion she had smoothed into her daughter's parched skin had done nothing to conceal the thick smell of death oozing from her pores. It was as if the child's body was releasing all its essential metals—returning them to the earth before—

"You didn't show up in court," Gus cut into her thoughts.

"I'm not leaving Krystaline's side. I told you that."

"I have sole custody, now."

"No conditions?"

"No conditions."

"You're going to take her to Seattle?"

"I'm not letting her die."

Krystaline whimpered and stirred restlessly.

"Gus," Chorie said desperately. "Look at her! Look at her, Gus! Does she look in any condition to travel?"

"Leave."

"Gus! Think about what you're doing, please! She's in so much pain. She wants to die, Gus. She would, if you'd let her. She's ready."

"You're fucking insane, woman. Leave or I'll call the cops."

The child gasped. Gurgled. Took three breaths and then her chest stopped moving. Chorie glued her eyes on her motionless daughter. Seconds passed. Gus approached, leaned over, put his hand under her nose. Krystaline sucked in the three more quick breaths.

"Cheyne-Stokes," Chorie said.

"Pardon?"

"The homecare nurse told me that pattern of breathing is called Cheyne-Stokes respiration. It often precedes dying."

"No!" Gus said, throwing the papers to the floor. "No!" He picked up his daughter, sat on the bed, and cradled her to his chest. "No! Krystaline! Krystaline! Daddy's here. Breathe!"

She was limp in his arms. Pale. Tiny. Thin. Nothing but bones. She shivered, gasped. Three more breaths and then nothing.

Chorie crept across the bed. She laid her head on Gus' shoulder. "Let her go," she whispered, reaching for her daughter's hand.

"No! No! Not now! I have a Christmas present for you, Kryssie. Just five more days. Five days. Please! Please! For Daddy."

CHAPTER 21

"How can I be so brave?" Chorie muttered.

"What's the matter?" Gus asked.

The baby flopped in her belly, strong forceful movements that could now be easily seen beneath the stretch of her shirt. Perhaps the baby would be born Christmas day.

"Krystaline's dying and I'm urging you to accept that fact. She's dying in your arms. I'm holding her hand. I'm so sad, yet so brave. I'm there for both of you."

"Krystaline's not dying, Chorie! Snap out of it! How did your session go with the doctor?"

"She's still insisting I'm crazy," Chorie said. "She wants to give me psychotropic drugs to cure my delusions. I won't take them."

"Why not?"

Chorie sighed. "At least not until the baby's born."

"Then you will?"

"Gus, they won't help me. It's not a delusion."

"Chorie, people who have delusions never believe they're delusions."

"Gus, I've come to realize Doctor Penny in Seattle is right. I'm experiencing another full-blown reality."

"No, Chorie. It just seems like that to you."

"Then why did the doctor recognize me? She asked where we'd met before. Gus, she's my counsellor in the other reality!"

"Come on, Chorie. Don't, please. People look familiar all the time."

"Because of alternate realities! Déjà vu, intuition, bad feelings, and bad vibes. The notorious inaccuracies and discrepancies of eyewitnesses. It's all because of bleed-through from other worlds, Gus! I've researched this. I'm convinced. I'm going back to Seattle."

"No. Definitely not! That doctor is in serious trouble. I've been following it on the internet. They've suspended his licence, Chorie. Stay away from him!"

"He's my only, hope, Gus."

"Try the medications, first, please. Just try them."

"They aren't going to work and I can't survive any longer with things the way they are. It will be a month before I'll be able to start taking them, and then weeks more before we find out they don't work. I won't last that long. Our marriage won't last that long. Maybe by that time Doctor Penny will be in jail and unable to help me. I'm packing. Taking the first flight out."

"I won't let you! That doctor is not only crazy, he's dangerous! Patients are saying he's offered to murder them as a way to get rid of one of their multiple lives. How fucking insane is that?"

"I won't let him murder me, Gus."

"He puts patients under without the benefit of an anaesthesiologist and without even a nurse present! Does brain surgery! You're not going, Chorie! You're not!"

"If Doctor's Penny's treatment doesn't help me I promise I'll try the medication."

"Chorie, sit!" Gus pointed to the black leather sofa. "Believe me; you are not experiencing another world! You're just stressed with work. Maybe second-guessing this pregnancy. And my tryst with Deanna obviously didn't help either—"

"Gus, stop it! I've researched delusions and I'm not psychotic; people who are don't function normally. I admit my emotional reactions are sometimes not appropriate, but otherwise…Gus, I can still take care of myself. I can prepare complicated tax returns. I can cook a supper. I can watch a soccer game, drive a car. I follow the news. Other than the emotional spill-over from my other life, I'm normal. Aren't I?"

"You think it's normal that you have two lives? That you believe your daughter is dying? That…."

"No! I don't believe that's normal! Gus, if you don't want to believe that is what's happening to me, at least believe that there's something going on in my brain that makes it seem that way to me. There's science behind that! MRI's show excessive firing of nerves in the part of the brain that governs things like dreaming and creativity. Adeline's medications won't stop that. Doctor Penny's treatment does!"

"How do you know his treatment will work?"

"I had an MRI done when I was in Seattle—"

"By Doctor Penny—who's crazy, Chorie!"

"I've been corresponding with some of the patients he's treated. They're happy with the results—no complaints."

"You're not going, Chorie. If need be, I'll have you declared insane and locked up."

"You want your baby born in an asylum?"

"Chorie."

"Just because your mother's insane, doesn't mean I am!"

"I know you don't like my mother, but she's not insane."

"She was, when you were a teenager. Although she prefers to call it an episode of 'nervous exhaustion'."

"How do you know about that?"

"You told me."

"I've never told anybody!"

"Oh…I guess you told me in my other life. Or, since you don't believe in my other life, I guess I'm psychic. Does that sit better with you? Psychic, rather than psychotic?"

"Are there…other things you know from your other life?" Gus asked slowly.

"I knew Stephen was a pompous ass and wasn't going to work out for you."

"Oh, yeah. I remember you saying that. What else?"

"Not everything I remember from that life is going to be the same in this reality. Like, Adeline being a psychologist, not a psychiatrist. It's only a twist of fate your mother was insane in both realities. Everything that can happen does. She could very well have been sane in one or both of my lives. Stephen could very well have been quite good at his work in this reality."

"I see."

"Some of Everett's Many Worlds will be very much like this one. Perhaps in one reality, you cough at three a.m. Tuesday and in a parallel universe, you don't. Other than that, everything's the same. However, there's also a vastly different world in which your grandfather was killed in the civil war and neither your father nor you were born."

"I know. That's the theory. Just theory, though, Chorie. Just theoretically meandering."

"With a solid scientific and mathematical base. Listen to me, Gus. You've taken advanced physics courses. You know what I'm saying. Now, tell me, would someone who is insane, be able to carry on this type of intellectual conversation with you? Do you think?"

CHAPTER 22

"I'm surprised you want to see me, considering all the bad publicity I've been getting lately," Dr. Penny chuckled. His voice was so smooth, his eyes so dark.

"Several things have happened lately that have me convinced you're right about what's going on," Chorie said. "I was scared if I waited much longer, you wouldn't be available to help me."

Dr. Penny shrugged. "Either way, life would go on, right?"

"Lives," Chorie corrected. "Many lives."

"Everything that can possibly happen."

"My husband didn't want me to come. He's scared you'll kill me." Chorie watched the doctor's face closely. She had has many misgivings as Gus, except she was much more desperate.

"You can believe whatever you want of the rumours out there."

"One of your patients, a 'Daniel', told me you offered to kill him as a means of getting rid of one of his lives for him."

"Like I said, believe what you want. I can't discuss other patients."

"In general terms, then, would murder seem like a viable alternative to you?"

"No. What would be the point? Consciousness would just carry on in alternate worlds where you didn't die. All you would be doing is cutting short a unique experience."

"You've never offered to kill a patient?"

"Look. The man asked me an emotional question and I responded with a logical answer, causing a major miscommunication. This man is not stable, if he were he wouldn't have been seeing me—a fact the Psychiatrists' Association seems willing to overlook. Daniel and I held a philosophical discussion on death and its place within the Many World's Theory. Chorie, professional associations are notorious for rejecting new ideas and methodologies. Always have been. Do you know the hoops Freud had to jump through to get anyone to even listen to his theories, let alone accept them? Back then, you had to get by the old man's club of the Catholic Church, as well. My work is too cutting edge for the establishment. It's deemed a sin to incorporate other sciences into the study of the human mind. It's why all branches of sciences falter and gasp. There's no one willing to unify man's knowledge. I'm fighting the system. Much evil will be spoken of me, by many well-respected men."

"I understand. I need to know what to expect if I go through with this treatment. It won't hurt the baby, will it?"

"I can make no guarantees, but there's no reason to expect it to."

"What will it be like after? Will I remember things?"

"My patients have reported full recall of the other life they've touched. Those memories, however, gradually fade and take on a dream-like quality."

"And I'll no longer have access to that life?"

"Some patients report a continuing feeling of kinship with those they met during their experiences. Some feel they can offer guidance and support to their other selves via their thoughts. Some feel they still connect while sleeping. None of them have found any of these effects disturbing."

"When I wake up from the anaesthetic, what will it be like?"

"Most patients report an initial feeling of disorientation, as if there's a time lapse. Generally they feel only a few hours are lost to them. Some though, can't remember the last few weeks in either life. It takes only a day or two, though, before they feel comfortable again. In all cases, the missing memories slowly return."

"Do those close to them notice any change?"

"From all reports, loved ones are very happy with the changes."

"What if something goes wrong? Has this treatment ever failed?"

"I'll be there on the other side should you need support."

"What about my other life?"

"I have no control over your other life. As far as I know it will continue on."

Krystaline would die. Society would judge the mother insane from grief and she'd spend the rest of her life in an institution, telling anyone who would listen she was living another life where she was still married, Krystaline still lived, and a new baby girl slept in the cradle. But that was okay. It's what she had wanted; she'd vowed she'd go crazy after the funeral. Leaving Gus free to blame her. Leaving him free to fall into Deanna's arms.

"Let's do it, Doctor Penny."

CHAPTER 23

"You will feel no pain," Dr. Penny hypnotically intoned. "You may smell garlic, a minor side effect of the anesthetic." She glanced at his hand. She could see the shape of the needle weaving deeper under her skin.

"Count backwards from ten," he instructed.

"Ten, nine…" The thick, clinging, taste of garlic coated the back of her throat. "Eight…" Lavender and garlic and cinnamon. Crayons and autumn leaves. Nickel. Tin. Garlic. Roses.

Chorie began to panic. The drugs weren't going to work. She was going to…"Sev…"

"We have to take the baby! Now! We're losing the heartbeat!"

"Gus!" Chorie screamed as pain gripped her abdomen.

"We'll have to put her out. The contractions are coming too quickly to administer a spinal. Scrub!"

"Sir? Sir, you'll have to leave. I'm sorry, sir. The husband has to leave."

"Are we set? It will be over soon, Chorie. The anaesthetic makes some people smell garlic. Count backwards from ten for me…"

"Will it hurt the baby? It won't hurt the baby will it? Ten, nine, eight, sev…" Garlic. Lavender. Tin. *Johnson's Baby Shampoo.*

~ * ~

Chorie kicked at the sheets binding her feet to the bed. "The baby," she whimpered.

"Ah, you're waking up!"

Chorie opened her eyes. Gus was standing in front of the window, a small bundle in his arms.

"Would you like to see your Christmas present?" he asked, pulling the blanket from the baby's face as he walked toward her.

"Is she okay?" Chorie asked.

"No, *she's* not," Gus said, shaking his head and smiling a small smile. "But *he* is."

"It's a boy?" Chorie said, struggling to sit. Pain ripped across her stomach and she lay back with a moan.

"That's what they say. I haven't checked for myself. I'll leave that to you."

"Krystaline will be so happy to have the brother she wanted."

The smile dropped from Gus' face. His eyes glazed. "Don't you remember?" he asked. His pace slowed. It was going to take him forever to get to her. She hoped it did. She hoped he never said what he was about to say.

She locked her eyes on his as he came nearer and nearer. Terror started at her toes, tingled up her legs, froze her tummy. Her breathing ceased; her heart slowed.

He glided toward her. Nestled next to her. Hugged the baby close. Keeping his sad eyes on hers, he slowly, slowly reached for her hand. Rubbed his thumb down her fingers. "Don't you remember, honey? Krystaline's dead."

ABOUT THE AUTHOR

Eileen Schuh lives in the remote northern boreal forests of Alberta, Canada. Drawing inspiration from the wilderness, she creates entire universes populated with fascinating charac-ters doing intriguing things.

Her interest in psychology dates back decades to her years as a psychiatric nurse. Her penchant for pondering Quantum Physics came later, when she needed something to contemplate while her hands were busy with the many repetitive and boring tasks of motherhood.

Schuh recently retired from a life of careers that varied from nurse to journalist to editor to business woman. She re-mains active in her adopted community of St. Paul and basks in the love and loyalty of an entire flotilla of family and friends. There's no doubt, however, that it's her grandchildren who are now the centre of her universe.

Schrödinger's Cat is her first published book and as such, is the realization of a childhood dream.

www.ingramcontent.com/pod-product-compliance
Lightning Source LLC
Chambersburg PA
CBHW051927220626
47052CB00003B/609